BILLY RAY PYLE'S STYLE

ISBN 0-89868-362-9–Library Bound
ISBN 0-89868-414-5–Soft Bound
ISBN 0-89868-363-7–Trade

A PREDICTABLE WORD BOOK

BILLY RAY PYLE'S STYLE

Story by Janie Spaht Gill, Ph.D.
Illustrations by Lori Anderson Wing

 ARO PUBLISHING

Everyone at school but Billy Ray Pyle dressed exactly alike, for that was the style.

Billy had shoes that were wild, crazy, and new. On Monday he wore his new shoes to school.

When Charlie Kazoo saw that very strange sight,

he called Billy aside to help set him right.

On Tuesday Charlie and Billy Ray
Pyle wore wide, baggy pants, their
own special style.

9

When Jimmy McKinny saw that
very strange sight,

he called his two friends aside to help set them right.

On Wednesday, Jimmy, Charlie, and Billy Ray Pyle wore tropical shirts, their own special style.

13

When Matthew MaCan saw that very strange sight, he called his three friends aside to help set them right.

15

On Thursday, Mattew, Jimmy,
Charlie, and Billy Ray Pyle wore

long, striped socks, their own
special style.

When Henry Hillway saw that very strange sight,

he called his four friends aside to
help set them right.

On Friday, Henry, Mattew, Jimmy, Charlie, and Billy Ray Pyle wore

bright, wide-rimmed hats, their own special style.

Today in that school, a sign sits on the shelf. It reads, "You are unique, so please be yourself."

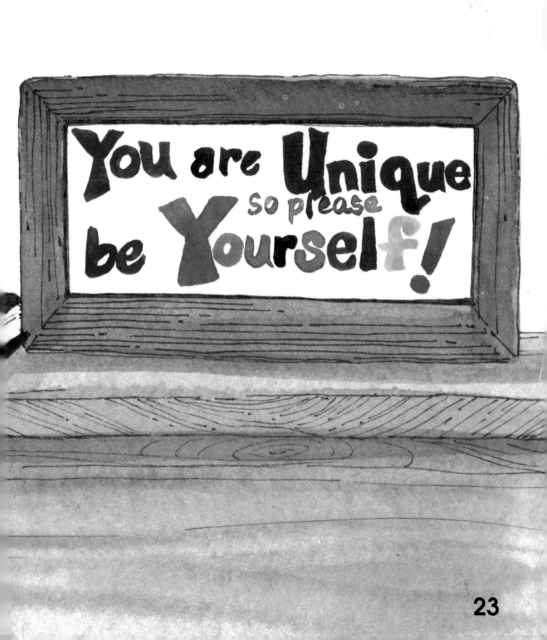

23